NICE
THINGS

BY

JAMES
FRANCO

✿

NICE
THINGS

BY

JAMES
FRANCO

❁

EDITED BY

SEAN LOVELACE AND MARK NEELY

NEW MICHIGAN PRESS

TUCSON, ARIZONA

NEW MICHIGAN PRESS

DEPT OF ENGLISH, P. O. BOX 210067

UNIVERSITY OF ARIZONA

TUCSON, AZ 85721-0067

<http://newmichiganpress.com>

Orders and queries to <nmp@thediagram.com>.

ISBN 978-1-934832-53-0. FIRST PRINTING.

Printed in the United States of America.

Design by Ander Monson.

CONTENTS

This book is for

Mark and Sean, whose work editing this collection
was relatively valuable. (Thanks for the coffee and
the semicolon help, guys!) I would also like to thank
McDonald's, moving pictures, war, and the sky. And
thank you Tom, for the aircraft carrier, hide and
seek, etc.

Proceeds from the sales of this work may benefit The Karen Beasley Sea Turtle Rescue and Rehabilitation Center.

"…underneath, everyone is living some other life you don't know about."

"There was a moon and it was on the water. I always see nice images like that but I don't know what to do with them."

—James Franco

We can't have nice things
in this artichoke-
painted room, sitting all itchy
and opera-esque, fat, obsolete,
horny for Sleater-Kinney.

The Seventies died for a reason.
Nothing ages
so fast as the futuristic—intercoms
and double-necked guitars,
you get me?

Sopranos have heart attacks at sixty.

Nothing ages so fast as a film
where the protagonist
tries to teach us a lesson.

Q: Your ninth book, *Nice Things by James Franco,* is a collection of linked stoemoirs (what you once called, "autobiographical stories in plotted verse"). Can you describe how this collection came together?

A: All I know is that when I needed McDonald's, McDonald's was there for me. When no one else was.

Q: Right, right…I think it's safe to say you like to push the literary envelope. In *Nice Things by James Franco,* you break the rules of traditional memoir—eschewing a traditional narrative arc for a more fragmented structure. You also move readers back and forth in time and emotional territory. And you switch point of view a lot, moving from first to third so intuitively and appropriately that you rarely jar the reader. So where'd you get your writing chutzpah?

A: Someone asked me if I was too good to work at McDonald's. Because I was following my acting dream despite all the pressure not to (or at least I felt pressure then, and maybe do now), I was definitely not too good to work at McDonald's. I went to the nearest Mickey D's and was hired the same day. I was given the late shift drive-thru position. I wore a purple visor and purple polo shirt and took orders over a headset. I refrained from reading Gogol on the job, but soon started putting on fake accents with the customers to practice for my scenes in acting class.

Q: *In Nice Things by James Franco,* various motifs are woven through the text, not unlike the patterns in a fine Persian rug. Which comes first for you: character or theme?

A: I had been a vegetarian for a year (or so) before working there because I was obsessed with River Phoenix, a staunch vegetarian—he actually cried on a date with Martha Plimpton (his girlfriend at the time—look it up!) when she ordered soft-shell crabs. But as soon as I got to McDonald's and was paying my own way, I started eating the cheeseburgers that were headed for the trash after being under the warming lamps for more than seven minutes. I would also sneak frozen apple bars and eat them in the freezer, still frozen—great with coffee.

Q: You mentioned reading. How does your reading life inform your writing? What are you reading now?

A: After a month, they allowed me to work the front counter during the day. Parents ordering for their children are the worst, and parents ordering for a group of children, like a sports team, are the devil. Some customers seem to think that paying for food entitles them to boss the service workers around, but if you're buying fast food, how much entitlement does that buy you? When you're paying a dollar for a burger, is it the end of the world if I accidentally forgot to take the mustard off the order? Sometimes they put me at the fry station, where you have to drop baskets of fries for people *who haven't even ordered yet*. It taught me a lot about the future.

Q: James, focus: *Nice Things by James Franco*, named for one of your father's phrases (he was always good with titles), is told in a maximalist style, while the next three books of stoemoirs, *113 Crickets*, *1970s: A Disaster Tale*, and *Anglo-Nubian Goats: A Disaster Tale* swirl around a minimalist style. What led to this transition?

A: I was treated fairly well at McDonald's. If anything, they cut me slack. And, just like their food, the job was more available there than anywhere else. When I was hungry for work, they fed the need. I still love the sincerity of the McDonald's hamburger. Maybe once a year, while out tuning a piano or cashiering at the local grocery (I'm quite tired. I'm on my feet the whole time. Suddenly you look in the mirror and you find out you're not 14 anymore. You're 29!) or spot-welding or writing Spam haiku (it's a thing—look it up!) or walking marathons (People say the marathon is 26.2 miles, it isn't. It's 20 miles first, sparks and sprinkles of pain [though it isn't suffering], and you rely on the homework, the fartlek/intervals, the hill-work [*Legs all minnows in a butter of shadow*, (Gertrude Stein)], the

long walks on Sunday listening to audio cookbooks; but
then comes the second race, the 6.2 miles, the suffering,
a tunnel, a cloudy tunnel that closes in, with lightning
spider webs on the walls [if you can imagine], and you
go to this place [I can't explain it, a cave? A lost cave
below an extinguished sea, on mars? (Plato)], this place...
far away...well, anyway, the marathon isn't one race of
26.2 miles: no, it's two races, two separate identities, one
walk of a tolerable pain, the other walk of—yes, I'll say
it—exquisite and existential *agony*.) or say you're out in
the middle of nowhere stargazing or heading home after
an exhausting day/night on a catfish pond, I'll stop by
a McDonald's and get a simple cheeseburger: light yet
succulent, airy and satisfying.

Or holding the mirror of ourselves
before everything, even Saturn's
unfeeling rings, even our memories
swirling through us like a Space
Odyssey where everything is terrible
or beautiful or both. We can't
have nice things unless we begin
to think of the constellations
not as mobiles hung for our pleasure
but as remnants

of devastating battles. Every time
I buy bread, strawberries to delicately
mangle, the satellites notice.
They carry me around so
quickly—

a boy skipping rocks over the lime
scum floating on the pond,

invisible.

Let us discuss the weather: a shimmering, glistening, twinkling sun in the western sky, gossamer, etc. Tendrils I suppose. Over there, a burbling sparrow (or possibly a wren). This weather is like a whimsical prank and I for one admire its pluck and verve and general good looks. Pretty much that's it. Let's move on, to James Franco, as he returns to America, to suck on Pop-Tarts all day while binge watching *The Sopranos*, *Battlestar Galactica*, *Mad Men*, and so on. One Tuesday he silences the TV and grabs a pen (Sharpie, blue) and scribbles out a detailed plan for spending the next two years on local, city buses. Just living the hobo life, listening to music, riding public transportation, munching on Pop-Tarts, passing out philosophical advice, polishing off fifths of whiskey, strutting crazy down the aisles with a bottle in hand…but James Franco can't locate his Sony Walkman, and, anyway, as time passes, music seems to have less and less impact on James Franco's soul. Life's like that, thinks James Franco, you get into something, really it moves you, and then it fades…like mint thinning, for example, that's really satisfying—thin those mints!—then who knows, just really ordinary, this emptiness roiling within your chest, same with animal husbandry or traffic engineering or making love against the rough bark of a tree—wow, exciting, wow, weeks of this and not so exciting, just twigs in your hair and rustling ivy in your underwear, who really knows…James Franco sighs, tosses aside the pen, opens a new box of

Pop-Tarts, takes a shower, puts on a suit the color of wet sand, and gets into advertising.

James Franco is the new man: they put him on soccer balls. First week, he's standing in front of his clients, crackling lights, looming white screen, his boss in the back of the room, the crouching shadow of a panther.

(Cartoon image of a large yellow skeleton key.)

James Franco yells out, "There are many more keys in the world than locks: SOCCER BALL!"

...

"SOCCER BALL!"

Moments drip by. The clunk and whir of air-conditioning. James Franco glances at his boss and then back to his clients.

(Cartoon image of a large, crackling fire.)

"One thing heats the body twice: SOCCER BALL!"

...

Moments, heavier now, like the meeting has developed seasons.

"SOCCER BALL!"

…

James Franco licks his lips and coughs. "See, um, if
you play soccer, you're, you know, running around and
sweating, so then the soccer ball is heating you once…
and then…later, if the soccer ball was used up or
deflated or whatnot, you could set it on fire and it would
heat you again—*One thing heats the body twice!*"

"SOCCER BALL!"

The clients stand. Raindrops lick the window glass, then
hum. James Franco considers poetry for the ninth time.

When the whole thing stinks
like a Christmas tree
air freshener (a month of Black
Fridays coming over the hills
like Hessians)
swaying crazily
from your rearview
as you screech off cursing
my stuttering soliloquies.

We could never give ourselves
entirely over to our bodies—

the ten million (billion?)
bacteria squishing
around inside us, sliming
our skins—Van Morrison
vibrating the woofer.

Though the sun did rise
confused behind the frosty
clouds and melted the grass
without instruction.

Though the moon would just appear
without a reason.

Multiflora rose blooms! Fireworks! *Shhhhhh…*a
rainfall…bright kudzu draped on the trees, telephone
lines, humped shapes of green: camels, curtains,
hippopotami and Volkswagens, shadowy rolling clouds
of leaf and vine. A cane toad squats on a fallen log. In
the sky: black funnels of starlings, twisting, flexing,
splotches of oil, scarves of smoke. Additional rain. A
large nutria swims from its den, leaves the roadside
pond, shakes off a spray of water, and then walks
into the left tire of a Subaru. Whoosh! (McDonald's
bag flung from rear window; french fries explode;
mallards waddle up and gorge…) What's in the wind?
Tumbleweed tumbling, rolling into a house, piling up,
blocking the doors. A teenager crawls out the bathroom
window; says, "What the fuck?" A Burmese python
swallows a Burmese python. Carp leap into the face of
a water skier. The All England Club leases and then
releases a hawk to patrol the skies above its Wimbledon
Championship. Pigeons scatter or die. People quaff
champagne. People nibble strawberries. People clap
politely, while James Franco sits on a grass mat in
southern Ho Chi Minh City (he's touring southern
Asia on stilts), trying dog for dinner, specifically Dog
Meatballs: ground up and wrapped in betel-nut leaves,
bits of cilantro and lemongrass, chewy and gray…James
Franco gnaws at the stringy meat and thinks about
taking a photo but doesn't take a photo, instead grabs
a nearby candle, hollows out its core with a spoon,

then secrets the slivers of meat inside. He thanks the restaurant owner. Mounts his stilts and lumbers into the forest. Butterflies flutter. Zebra mussels settle onto a Diet Mountain Dew can. A Great Lake sighs. A woman opens a screen door and calls to a cat and calls to a cat and calls to a cat, but the cat never comes.

If we've forgotten how to build a house
in the woods or start a horse
without a button.

Blame Pop-Tarts and toaster ovens,
Apple and Google, Walmart and Jeopardy,
Gogol probably. Blame the Clintons
and their aw-shucks murdering of the past.

We can't have nice things
if every answer is a question,
every question a howler,
every howler a vainglorious
host—

Category: *Disappearances*.
Answer: *Who the fuck is Gogol?*

In fourth grade we built a replica
of Abraham Lincoln's cabin. We ran in
circles on the blacktop, crossing the finish, over and over,
without knowing.

Driving toward an alcoholic mecca
in the Chevy Cavalier,
saying, *If you bought it, a truck brought it,*
and *Perfect is the enemy of good,*
and *A word too much repeated / falls out of being.*

Best not to say anything,
to let the space between your ears
swell like a nail bomb

as bank branches
blur in the windows
and the McDonald's flashes dimly
and workers in green hard hats
finish our brilliant society—
scrubbing red scribblings
from the wall. We can't have nice things

unless we're willing to watch
a gang of woodpeckers chip away at the soffits,
willing to let the motherfucker fall.

In an adaptation (some critics would even imply plagiarism) of his mentor, Toshiko Takaezu, James Franco attempts a revolutionary method of firing a triptych of copper plates at high temperatures in saggers (clay containers he keeps in the lambing barn) but the saggers explode, injuring a nearby ewe. In disgust James Franco marches to the kitchen, empties half a two-liter Diet Sprite, and fills the bottle with thick Monrovian wine.

Amongst the flowers (dandelions), dusk I assume, the light tumbling like a shouted soliloquy down a kitchen drain, etc., James Franco puts down his biography (Axl Rose, born in Lafayette, Indiana—look it up!) and sits and drinks from the Diet Sprite bottle and thinks of sculpting, magnificent sculpting, scenes from the past, with both historical and psychological truthfulness!

And the moon coughs along the sky.

—*oh moon won't you drink with me?*

James Franco sighs, for the moon will not drink. What good is the moon? Moon. Moon! Bloom...gloom! Buffoon! What a silly word. Silly gray rock, really, probably basalt, or maybe, maybe marble...James Franco stews, stirs and stews over his inability to sculpt because of recent arsenic and mercury poisoning (from

a part-time taxidermy job at the local museum), but still
the moon just stares at him, empty.

—*Moon! I demand you bring me a wheelbarrow full of
bronze! A, a…winged woman…an allegory of sacred and
profane…love?…I don't know, found…found objects,
Batman, shrubbery…I'm intoxicated.*

The moon sits high and silent, a clapperless bell.

Whatever, James Franco snorts and takes a large swig
and in the tilted wink of the Diet Sprite bottle notices
a smeary, shimmering reflection: Ah! Ah ha! James
Franco smiles. James Franco smiles (not so unlike the
smile of certain tree frogs or Mona Lisa or more likely
of exhausted orchestra players when they finally lower
their instruments and quietly exhale)—for there they
drink together as one, in a wobbly, green, pebbled,
plastic, poetic image: the wine (with Diet Sprite), the
moon, James Franco…

If your script is always changing, being
handed over to the hacks in Palo Alto,
the Paleo, ExxonMobil.

A script should be impenetrable,
like the Bible. Like pre-colonial
forests where a squirrel could travel
from Illinois to the ocean
without touching the ground.

A script should have
two bloody plot points
like this one.

Q: Was there a lot of plotting involved when you worked on *Nice Things by James Franco?*

A: For structural concerns, I turn to Nature. Pond scum, rivers, clouds, the rain. As I mentioned over brunch, the drippings of memory remain after a steady rainfall, drifting here, drifting there, a dusting of bloblets (a word I coined), that keen yet timeless odor, a lingering (much like the ribbons of a sneeze, at least to my thinking). Sometimes I'd sit coughing for weeks over one solitary sentence. I like to linger and had to fight that. I had to learn to amputate. For example, I went way too far with the tortoise and whale research. I tossed three chapters off the train (a total of 930 pages), just had the window open and whoosh! Another example: in the last chapter of *Nice Things by James Franco*, there's a scene where James Franco and Walt Whitman and The Muffin Man are attending the Indiana State Fair, having a shouted conversation in the rattling car of a descending roller coaster. I wrote fourteen remembrances of that conversation, and none of them felt right (they had no reality, basically). So, what was the solution? Here's a little writing tip for you: there was none. Only confusion. Art is a songless bird, a gas station coffee—a void. A lot of the manuscript I couldn't figure. I would sigh and gnash, gnash and sigh, and then take the whole ugly mess over to John Bonham's flat. Or I might run it by Phil Collins (this was in 1968, '69—both musicians were knocking about the West End, pounding beers, scarfing bags of chips, relentlessly cleaning their drum kits, all that). I'd just run it by drummers, you know, someone to help with the pacing and the rhythm. A collection isn't just a random gathering of words. It's an organism, a thing, like a Nintendo or a draft horse or, well, a musical album. So, yeh for me, drummers. John was a bricklayer (this is why he could drum with his hands—they were basically calloused iron) and so often I couldn't locate him and if I did locate him he might be on a high rooftop and I'm not going to be cartwheeling about any high rooftop like a teenager. So then I'd try to locate Phil, but Phil Collins, in case you don't know (and I can't see why you would), was a father figure to most everyone and so was usually off counseling Mike or Tony, even Pete sometimes, so I'd give up and just sort of walk in aimless circles for hours (my legs now numb) and meander my way home (usually with a high fever) and work on the manuscript, outside on the park bench, as I said, in a chilly, relentless, London rainfall. (The toes of my feet now frozen and I would honestly be thinking about the hospital, not literature.) Utterly alone. Basically, I learned what not to do. So that's what I know about planning. Anyway, I quit writing *Nice Things by James Franco*. I simply had enough. I gave the madness of the manuscript away, to a random passerby. "Written words are often smarter than their writers," a wise man once said to me. Though I can't recall who it was, or why.

Unless you lie down. Unless the elephants
agree on a voluntary buy-back and the ornamental
gunstocks made from their faces.

It's more than a fetish,
shitting in the Earth's mouth
every night, but how gorgeous

the brick chimneys look
talking smack to the sky. When I was young
I didn't notice this crap.
I did laps.

I drove north with father and blew away
a few terrorist bears and drank
my second beer and thought Axl Rose
was inside me.

We can't have nice things.
The sun has decided.

James Franco mail ordered a monk. The monk was the son of a flea trainer, who was the son of a flea trainer, who was again the son of a man who professionally trained fleas. "The blood of the flea is within our soul," the monk told James Franco over Pop-Tarts (this was in North Dakota, on a small flea farm), but James Franco looked away, replied with a word he just made up (*hoffenslop!*), bought two rabbit hounds, ran them in circles, competed with them nationally (his official record was 1-33), and then lost both dogs in a California mudslide. "What is your deal?" the monk scolded him over Skype. "Don't be so ponderous. The flea is your destiny." James Franco wept and rented a Cessna 152 (the same model once eaten by a Frenchman?). Here was his deal: James Franco admires mounds of trash (sculptures to his thinking) and cobwebs and loud neckties and photos of windows and plum blossoms and micro-dermabrasion facial creams and he will not remove any of them, ever. A local grocer once labeled him an unraveling ball of yarn, but he more resembles a gray squirrel: A.) not daunted by cold weather; B.) so weary after swimming in the ocean he can be caught by hand; C.) rushes and leaps through life at full speed, no means safe from falling, but usually managing to catch hold somewhere, often by only a single toe…Ah, **the suspense! Image: Beige building, fog. Zoom to a** room full of people who have disappointed their monks and need to talk it over. *Hi, everyone, my name is James*

Franco and I struggle with silence and the Italian language.
Moving on…commence the metaphor! The metaphor
is now commencing: writers and flea trainers are very
similar. Image: Chevy Cavalier, taking flight. Printed
words are a form of mildly intelligent insect, meant to
crawl about us with some wonder and knowledge—but
no matter how carefully the insect is trained, it is hard
to guess what may happen once it is released into, into
the…Ah, suspense! *Franco Traffic, Cessna Five Three
Two Nine Bravo is on the ramp, taxiing to the end of
runway one one, Franco.* The plane clips two pelicans
(or possibly, swans), spins, jolts, bumps, bounces into
a heat thermal, fire from fuel, fire from electrical…
ahhhhhhhhhhhhhh…sometimes you might spiral
within another spiral, and this is never good…blackout:
James Franco surfaces and coughs. Swims to shore. Buys
a bus ticket. *Jabberwocky! Jabberwocky! Jabberwocky!*
go words blabbering crazy into the frigid, morning
air, breath visible I suppose, oversize muck boots,
perspiration, wind through clothing, winter moon a
glowing balloon etc., etc., as James Franco shovels pile
after pile of flea manure with a teaspoon.

When I close my eyes a thousand short films
spin their reels—my crimes, one
by one, against women, against men and land,
my failures to act, my insistence on laughing
at terrible jokes, my indiscretions
with animals, the monster
peeling off my face,

revealing my face. There I am in a field,

or standing abaft of the *USS Enterprise*,
grinning like a tom, like madness itself,
leading the guests to the bedroom

where they pile their coats,
a strange orgy
of coats which later that night
we fondly remember.

Q: That's interesting what you say about elephant management, but you're now a writing professor as well. I know a lot of writers who feel that teaching saps them of energy, that it forces them to think too analytically about what is essentially an intuitive and mysterious process, and that the constant exposure to student writing deadens their own delight in language. How do you strike a balance between teaching and writing?

A: Ah, this issue of balance is like the holy veil for writers: academic life's no picnic of pomegranates, but I've found if your horse is running good, the flowers will one day bleat like bells from the cold manure (if you'll excuse the cliché)…So there you go. Now, the administrative side of it all, that's harder. Committees, for example. Or issues with people using the printer as a copier. The printer isn't a copier. So the writing sags. When I first started teaching, I kept beating myself up about it. I would go home and grab saplings, jump onboard, swing wildly until the trees snapped in half. (It made me feel better, I don't why.) All of this would delay the writing of a poem or a story by two, sometimes three days and no one was there to guide me, no wise sage to say something like, "Hey, James Franco, you sleep in the rain on a sandbar long enough and you begin to enjoy the act of sneezing." And I was keeping small children at the time, as I mentioned earlier. I remember reading that when his kids were

young, Raymond Carver would hole up in a local bar
for twelve or fifteen hours just to write a first draft.
I know that desperation. Sometimes I'll organize a
writer's colony and publicize it and accept funding
and applications and then, at the very last moment,
I'll cancel the entire colony. You know why? So I can
attend the colony, alone. (Fun fact: much of *Nice Things
by James Franco* was written by headlamp.) Just little
tricks of time management. Writing while showering.
Holding office hours on a Segway. Hiring five young
personal assistants. Things like that. You know, teaching
is a critical part of my identity. You tell people you're a
teacher, they understand. You say *writer* and they look
at you like you just asked to borrow their Blow Pop.
I'm fortunate in that I teach a lot of nursing courses in
addition to creative writing. Do you know what nurses
call a coronary artery bypass graft? A cabbage! Isn't that
weird? What about a motorcycle? They call them *donor-
cycles*. Those people are messed up—seriously, nurses
are *messed up*, I should know (I'm licensed in four
states)—the hours are long, long and hard, like writing,
like art… And I tell those nursing students the same
thing I tell all the young artists, what I wish someone
long ago had taken the time to tell me: "Listen, listen
carefully," I say. "Every dark cloud has a dropped bowling
pin. Brush yourself off, pick up that howling din and the
lightning will grin like lemonade…" So there you have it.

Rivers have their own rhetoric.
Out in the current their argument
becomes clear. We can't have
nice things without knowing
the trails, some brambly, some so low-
ceilinged you have to crash through them
crouching and compromised, all elbows
and knees. Then there's the question
of scat. Can it kill me or not?

Two guys with limps and bad teeth
follow the tracks behind the drug
store, looking for a nurse/godmother—suffering
like television
from a lack of imagination.

The locks clunk in my current
bubble. Even so such encounters
make my skin boil over.

They go on forever
in either direction.

Q: One of the things that impresses me most about *Nice Things by James Franco* is the voice of its narrator, James Franco. How did you find his voice?

A: I test drove—on a moped—numerous voices and characters (at least 14, including Butterworth, a shy Chilean veterinarian) before I found James Franco. I remember the day well, October 4, 1957: Sputnik had winked/winked at the earth and far below I had just gifted the lighting director of my penultimate vampire play a silver cigarette case and this phrase just popped into my head: *James Franco.* But one sentence into James Franco's story, I knew I was onto something; it was that immediate. To me, James Franco sounds both frightened yet curious, jaded yet perfumed, furious yet box office, small yet sly, worldly yet doorstep, sinewy yet vulnerable, a child and simultaneously an old man, a man who stinks of hazelnut relish and jazz, and whose left eye is covered by a colorful, bedazzled bandana. James Franco also displays stoicism—a quality I admire in farm animals but one that ultimately signifies repressed emotions. I should know. These emotions are there inside, percolating in my throat. I'm sure it is the same with many artists. (Fun fact: I collect graduate degrees, box turtles, log cabins, and regret.) And surely James Franco's deadpan, shall-we-say-noir reportorial voice is a way for him to temper those internal struggles so they don't gurgle and pop and then again gurgle to the surface. But then, sometimes, the world is too much with James Franco, and his voice cracks. That's when James Franco is forced to observe his surroundings with a certain poetic beauty. James Franco needs to see the beautiful, almost as much as the reader needs for James Franco to see it. In the middlemost images of *Nice Things by James Franco*, James Franco needs to see those wobbling pale breasts, those rings of Saturn spiraling wildly into the desert, those terrorist bears working the oil rig, that ocean and the leftover mayonnaise, the Chevy Cavalier and the tiny grains of sea salt, the serious world and the World Series, and, more importantly, those lambing ewes, bleating madly as they gallop along slick blood and the flying shrapnel of an exploding sculptor's kiln…Ah, darkness! That's at the heart of my voice. No one saved James Franco that night, no, so James Franco finds a way to save himself by creating light from darkness, if only so James Franco can last another day.

The best movies end with a damaged hero.
The best weddings open the bar—imagine a film
set without a pharmacy just down the street.

The best science makes me
cling to my statue of Mary, singing "John Henry," boring
into the future, timid, ham-handed,
enraged by the smallest waylay.

Experiments conducted over several millennia
have concluded dry weddings aren't any fun.

The best things in life are free

for the guests. My drunk uncle suggests
the best things in life are beneath
the bride's dress. We can't have nice
things through this haze.

If John gets there first,
he ruins the story.

James Franco crouched inside the horse, the darkness
like the darkness when the house lights go down, drawn
on forever. Near his left ear was a short wooden handle.
All he had to do was turn the handle counterclockwise.
All he had to do was step out and reveal himself.

"All I have to do is step out and reveal myself," he
thought.

But not yet. He was enjoying the solitude. He was
beginning to use the darkness, like a feeding bat, like the
plummeting stewardess in James Dickey's "Falling" uses
the time/space before her inevitable death—turning
in the wind, dictating her romance novel, carefully
removing each piece of the stifling uniform.

James Franco has already shed his uniform. Sitting
in this cramped position, a position of prayer almost,
would have been impossible in the stiff jeans and
woolen jackets of his former life. After a few days of
squatting, nude, he could differentiate the scents from
his body's various crannies—the earthen perfume of
the armpit, the rich, sweet musk of the groin, the fungal
banquet of the feet. To pass the time, he thought of first
times, trees he had conquered. He thought of Eighties
television. He thought of his friend Efrain, the line
cook, who cut off a finger during the lunch rush, threw
the severed digit in his pocket, and politely asked the

manager if he could leave a little early. This was the type of man James Franco was becoming.

The soldiers paced outside. He heard their voices, distorted by the thick siding of the horse's hull. It reminded him of his first apartment, the whispered arguments of the Vietnamese couple next door. James Franco's ear pressed hotly to the wall. He sensed the troops' inherent wariness. He knew the *U.S. Government Counterinsurgency Guide* (2009) was practically inscribed on the inside of their skulls. Some of them, perhaps, had never read *A California Childhood*. But in this hell of dust and burning waste, how could they help but be seduced by the delicate woodwork of the horse's mane, the magnificent hooves, the nostrils frozen in a terrible exhale? James Franco listened to their murmurings, confident he sat inside the one thing that could save them. All he had to do was step out and reveal himself.

"All I have to do is step out and reveal myself," he thought.

But not yet.

We can't have nice things
thinking only of tortoises
and smarter computers.

Which way to the dazzlement?
Who led us into this boredom, this battle?

These old soldiers drenching
pale pancakes in Mrs. Butterworth's,
these pale politicians under their government
hair.

What awful charisma he must have had.

There are more things between turtles
and Watson...

I looked them up.
Microbe extinction, micro black holes
opened up by the Hadron Collider,
giant viruses trapped in the permafrost.
Vaticide, omnicide, ecocide,
etc.

James Franco kneels in an alley by a metal garbage can
(the air smells of dead rat, moldy dill, the gouged eyes
of potato) and fingers the waxy bundle in his pocket
and nibbles at a shrunken apple; he thinks, "Few fruits
are cultivated as extensively as the apple–probably only
the grape has a broader range and I can't think of one
fruit with a deeper, more complex mythos (look it up!),
but yet again the historical ramifications of…" *I wonder
what's in the wax paper?*

An hour earlier a wiry man with a splotchy face had
approached James Franco, saying, "This is a sandwich.
Hold it for me. I will be back."

Ah, there go the parade balloons!

And over there some goats in their finery! Wait a
minute, those are horses. James Franco specifically
wants to see the goats.

And off nearby the celebratory cannons, not so unlike
thunder or the heartbeat echoing in the ears, the
throbbing blood, the interdependence of man, Nature,
the universe…though of course Nature has no real
philosophy, thinks James Franco, as he gnaws at the
apple core, It makes no judgments and writes no books
or scripts for situational comedy pilots. Only we do
that. Really we cannot look to nature for… *The bundle*

*feels heavy for such a small sandwich. And a bit cold, and
certainly an odd request to hold it, though James Franco
knows really nothing of the local customs or cuisine.*

Ah, more balloons! They drift in the high, blue sky…
red, green, yellow, a dance of air and light…They
form a sort of constellation, their shifting dots. James
Franco smiles in wonder, then frowns: a very annoying
constellation indeed—there goes Taurus, no Leo, no, no
Leo Minor—ah the cursed wind!—now it's simply an
enormous stuffed rabbit frying an egg.

The man returns, breathing hard, his face now even
redder, a world map of splotches. "Hand me that
sandwich," he huffs. "Take this one."

One wax paper bundle, two soggy wedges of bread—
exchanged. James Franco examines the sandwich: a
crumpled ball of onion smothered in something that
smells like motor oil. James Franco tosses it into the
garbage can and scampers off to find the goats.

Archduke Franz Ferdinand of Austria is jostling about
the back seat, leaning as the car rounds a tight city
bend of Sarajevo, while struggling with the belt of his
scabbard and sucking on the left breast of Sophie, his
wife. She's gained weight recently and her breasts are
huge, pale, white, wobbling globes. Franz Ferdinand

finds them magnificent. He slurps and grapples and falls, the ostrich feather of his helmet somehow lodged in her silver necklace, the car creaking and swaying, Sophie's dress billowing up, blue and white, lace and satin, itchy corners and flowery frills and glowing wedges of pale, perfumed skin…Franz wrestles himself deeper into the layers, inhales and shuts his eyes, feels he's letting go, tumbling, spinning free, into a roaring, crashing, pummeling ocean wave…The car halts.

James Franco—many streets away—locates the goats in their finery!

POP! POP! POP!

World War One begins.

We can't have nice things
slapping our tails on the wall,
rehashing old tussles
in grimy hotels while the economy
goes in the shitter.

If we can never sit still,
never hear the almost invisible
sound of a moth thrashing
under the lampshade,
never lie without tongues
sticking weirdly out of our mouths,

drawing spaceships and cumbersome
whales, breeching, falling,
for nothing,
drawing things we know
we can never have.

My parents jump from their beds
and stumble naked through the house
throwing nickels at our faces. Their nakedness

changes, gets lackadaisical, loopy,
looks all the way back, loses races, stoops
to the floor, solicits
the opinions of mayors. There

are no snow women dashing
on the lawn. Mom screams
at my sister for going out in that skirt.

We can't have nice things.

I climb through a second story
window as heaven's launch codes decay
in impenetrable cases.

I make my way through the snow.

Above western France James Franco tumbled (more sucked out actually) from a C-82 cargo plane and spinning, spinning, through strands of torn cotton, whirls of luggage-shaped clouds, flakes of snow, soups and footballs and marshmallows and wispy, white ropes like the starting cords of mowers, etc., etc., spinning, falling (140 mph now) and down below is another James Franco and below him another James Franco and another James Franco and another James Franco and another James Franco and another James Franco— imagine a flashing mobile in the sky (though devoid of wires, obviously), abstract shapes, some spray of heavy coins (or maybe horseshoes?) flung down from the heavens, tumbling, spinning, falling:

France? wondered the first James Franco. *I hope they have the fizzy water. The fizzy water is never the same elsewhere. Ah, France. So special, and don't they know it… the odd paradox is that France thinks it's the tutor to the world, yet it has never really believed it can be imitated.* "What are your thought on the paradox?" he yelled out to the second James Franco, spiraling far below.

This was of course absurd: to parachute is an incredibly loud activity. And anyway the second James Franco was wondering about Dostoevsky. Dostoevsky had seen him win a few kopeks one evening at the roulette table and thought James Franco had a system. James Franco had

no system. He just drank white wine from a coffee mug
and played all the red numbers for no reason greater
than he liked apples, especially Bismarcks (which
are Australian and damn near impossible to find at a
reasonable price). Nevertheless, coatless and shivering
in the hissing snow since he'd lost all his outer clothing
to gambling, Dostoevsky stalked James Franco all over
St. Petersburg. Finally, one day in the Café Babushka,
James Franco exploded: "There is no system! It's math.
You lose because it's math! No one in the world can
defeat math! It's like Time or Bob Costas—it cannot be
defeated! Believe me, believe me"—here James Franco
dropped to one knee while his face fell into an agonizing
state of self-combustion—"I've tried…believe me…"

Dostoevsky was moved. He was just about to ask James
Franco if he could borrow money for a cup of tea (it was
for roulette), but seeing such a forlorn James Franco in
his dark ṣamghāti (a type of robe preferred by Buddhist
monks of eastern Japan) and his camouflage New
Balance running shoes, Dostoevsky felt great pity, so
kept silent and went home to lightly edit a novella.

The third James Franco wandered his tongue over
his second molar—it throbbed from eating so much
popcorn at Comic-Con.

The fourth James Franco touched a long, red, rumpled
scar beneath his nipples and wondered about Brown
Blob (it was actually a mammoth), as it neared over
the tundra grass. (A Pliocene memory Pliocenely
remembered...) James Franco thought BROWN
BLOB OUCH STICK ROUND STICKY JUICE
SOUND SOUND FIRE BLOB YOW!

*House, house...*the fifth James Franco wondered, then to
that other, much different word, *home, home...will I ever
return? And where is it?*

The sixth James Franco wondered if Napoleon even
opened the cheese basket.

The seventh James Franco wondered about Baudelaire,
Genet, Celine, and Batman.

The eighth James Franco had finances on his mind,
specifically a bounced check and a faulty clutch on a
Subaru...

The ninth James Franco wondered this: VISUAL
MATCH-CUT ACTION VISUAL MATCH
CUT EXTENDED MATCH DISSOLVE CUT
SMASH CUT STEADICAM CUT MOTIVATED
LIGHTING FLASHBACK REALISTIC SOUND
CUT WIDE-ANGLE PAN VISUAL-MATCH
CUT BALANCE IMBALANCE CUT.

(A V of geese slid by his spinning form, horns blowing.)

The tenth James Franco pulled on his ripcord and
pulled on his ripcord and pulled-on-his ripcord!

Not really wondering much about anything at all.

It all comes down to a clerical error,
a fairy tale misunderstood as meaning
anyone can do it. No one can do it.

Blood pours through us
like storm through a sewer
and a few palsied leaves
shiver in the squall.

It's like left-handed pitching—
every so often a splitter
gets away. Every so often
the gods throw a hurricane
at a village of shanties,
throw an earthquake at the
World Series.

We can't have nice things
digging through rubble
in these bodies
that aren't even ours.

SEAN LOVELACE lives in Indiana, where he directs the creative writing program at Ball State University. His latest collection is about Velveeta and published by Bateau Press. He has won several literary awards, including the *Crazyhorse* Prize for Fiction. He likes to run, far.

MARK NEELY is the author of *Beasts of the Hill* (winner of the FIELD Poetry Prize) and *Dirty Bomb*, both from Oberlin College Press. He has been awarded fellowships from the NEA and the Indiana Arts Council and his poems have appeared in *Gulf Coast, Indiana Review, Boulevard, Columbia Poetry Review*, and elsewhere.

❃

COLOPHON

Text is set in a digital version of Jenson, designed by Robert Slimbach in 1996, and based on the work of punchcutter, printer, and publisher Nicolas Jenson. The few titles here are in Futura.

✻

NEW MICHIGAN PRESS, based in Tucson, Arizona, prints poetry and prose chapbooks, especially work that transcends traditional genre. Together with DIAGRAM, NMP sponsors a yearly chapbook competition.

DIAGRAM, a journal of text, art, and schematic, is published bimonthly at THEDIAGRAM.COM. Periodic print anthologies are available from the New Michigan Press at NEWMICHIGANPRESS.COM.

CPSIA information can be obtained
at www.ICGtesting.com
Printed in the USA
FSOW02n1759010316
17335FS